'And Guess Who He Was With?'

First published in 2013 by
Liberties Press
7 Rathfarnham Road | Terenure | Dublin 6W
Tel: +353 (1) 405 5701
www.libertiespress.com | info@libertiespress.com

Trade enquiries to Gill & Macmillan Distribution
Hume Avenue | Park West | Dublin 12
T: +353 (1) 500 9534 | F: +353 (1) 500 9595 | E: sales@gillmacmillan.ie

Distributed in the UK by
Turnaround Publisher Services
Unit 3 | Olympia Trading Estate | Coburg Road | London N22 6TZ
T: +44 (0) 20 8829 3000 | E: orders@turnaround-uk.com

Distributed in the United States by
Dufour Editions | PO Box 7 | Chester Springs | Pennsylvania 19425

ISBN: 978-1-907593-59-8
2 4 6 8 10 9 7 5 3 1

A CIP record for this title is available from the British Library.

Printed by Bell & Bain Ltd., Glasgow

'And Guess Who He Was With?'

Liz Cowley

To Donough and Katy

And with thanks to my agent, Jonathan Williams

Contents

I. Getting Together   9

First date   11

Blind date   12

Oh yes, he fancies you   13

Clueless   14

Girls together   16

Dinner dates   17

The nonsense of opposites   18

The height of passion   19

'And guess who he was with?'   20

Valentine's Day   21

Confidence   22

Trust   23

The optimist and the pessimist   24

It's worth the journey   25

II. Getting Low   27

Too young to compromise   29

Cheating?   30

A friend cries on my shoulder   31

Plateau   33

One lie too many   34

We find out in the oddest ways   35

You must think I'm stupid   37

He doesn't notice   39

'I'm not your slave'   40

If only we knew from the start   41

III. Getting Out   43
  'Sorry – it's over'   45
  'Sorry, I'm too knackered'   47
  'We can still be friends'   48
  One-way traffic   49
  A cautionary tale   50
  Why did you come back?   51

IV. Getting Hitched   53
  Too much planning   55
  He won't change   57
  Does he see you as a wife or a mother?   58
  A husband's complaint   59
  Beware of marrying an author   61
  Not now   62
  Silence, please   63
  I'd love to say 'I love you'   64
  Things I despair of   65
  Please don't be honest   66
  My husband's girlfriend   68
  Sex could be worse   69
  Sex or chocolate?   71
  I love you just the way you are   72
  Thank you   73

V. Getting Mad   75
  Why bother asking?   77
  House of horrors   79
  Clothes shopping   81
  Family rows   83
  Do you have a neighbour like this?   85
  Don't smile if you're about to be nasty   86
  'Just bring a bottle'   87

Attention-seekers 88

Time to kill 89

Doers and leavers 91

Your local 93

Round robins 94

Teenagers in your place abroad 95

Pet hate 96

VI. Getting Harassed 97

Saturday evenings 99

'What are you doing today?' 100

The joys of family holidays 101

The green-eyed monster 105

Could you cope without them? 106

Does your daughter long to have a pony? 107

Conundrum 109

'Do you think he's right for me?' 110

VII. Getting Depressed 111

Psychiatrists 113

Why are we so beastly to ourselves? 115

Your time is up 116

Oui, je regrette beaucoup 117

Self-doubt 119

Why put things off? 120

The simplest things 121

VIII. Getting On A Bit 123

A huge pleasure 125

A huge disappointment 126

Flirts 127

Cougar 128

'Are you a Granny?' 129

First time I've met her   130
Warning   131
Cocktail parties   132
Wandering off   133
You're in my space   134
'Do you remember?'   135
Surprise, surprise   136
My parents   137
My mother's death   138
A happy ending   139

I

Getting Together

'Do you think he fancies me?'

First date

I glance at you, but only glance,
then watch the indicator.
Well, that's what people always do
when in an elevator.

We reach the ground, and now I look:
not bad at all, I think;
how nice, you think the same of me
and ask me for a drink.

Blind date

'Do you think he fancies me?'

'I've no idea, but can't you tell?'

It's odd when women cannot spot
the signs that others know so well.

It surely comes as no surprise –
the clues are always in the eyes;

the first and clearest way to tell,
the second and the third as well.

'Just look at him, it's bound to show.
If not, alas, the answer's no.

Or maybe you're in need of glasses?
That could, of course, mean fewer passes.'

Oh yes, he fancies you

You see it in his eyes, a slight surprise –
alert to what you say and what you do.

You see it in the stillness of his eyes –
a steadiness of gaze provides a clue.

And so it is with posture, lest one move
might make you pause or somehow not approve.

He may well be a listener, maybe not,
but listen in he will, and quite a lot.

You note a pleasant tension in the air –
it's obvious a certain bond is there.

You'll see his interest, recognise that look
that starts the pages turning in a book.

The signs are strong; he's handed you the power
to change his world, and yours, within the hour.

The evidence is clear; it's up to you,
it's yours to choose just what, or not, to do.

Clueless

We're on a train to Putney.
I'm squashed up next to you.
You're filling in a crossword,
there's one word left to do.

You're puzzling, scribbling, frowning –
you're stuck on that last clue.
And suddenly I guess it,
and can't help telling you.

'A wild and poisonous flower'.
Which one? I thought I knew.
You didn't – you'd been struggling
since leaving Waterloo.

But should I try and tell him,
or would it spoil his fun?
And talking while commuting
is normally not done.

But then he banged his fist down,
I noticed his frustration.
And now's the time to tell him –
I'm off at the next station.

'Try hemlock,' I suggested.
'Oh, yes!' he said, delighted,
then filled it in and chatted
until we both alighted.

And still we're always chatting,
we've been a pair for ages –
and still there's not a cross word
when sharing crossword pages.

It's funny what attracts you
to somebody who's new.
I knew we'd be an item –
you hadn't got a clue.

Girls together

Shared flats so often seem to be
a breeding ground for jealousy.
There's always someone with no date
resenting that you're out so late,
or else with someone in your bed,
whom they would like in theirs instead,
or always moaning when you're there
you leave the kitchen cupboard bare
and don't take out the rubbish bin
or care what state the flat is in,
or worse, in whom you can't confide
because they'll take the other side,
or plot to steal your chap from you
as flatmates often tend to do.
I've very often wondered whether
we girls should ever live together.
Shared flats so often seem to be
a place to make an enemy,
instead of one for making friends.
So often it's where friendship ends.

Dinner dates

You're out with him – it's going well,
you like him, he likes you.
Then let him pay, you'll have your day
to settle up for two.

In two minds? Vaguely like your date?
A bit, but not that much?
This time chip in a bit of it,
or, better still, go Dutch.

You may not see the chap again,
or want to keep in touch,
so share the bill, it shows goodwill,
and half won't cost that much.

Don't fancy him? Then why not pay,
and walk away with pride?
The fellow may refuse of course,
but then, at least, you've tried.

And better still, he'll get the hint
and guess he's been rejected,
but find your gesture generous –
though somewhat unexpected.

Let him pay, or pay him off,
or pay an equal share,
but let men pay, and all the time?
Oh, girls, that's most unfair.

The nonsense of opposites

It's said that opposites attract.
The opposite is surely true.
Can *you* think why you'd like a guy
at odds with what you feel and do?

Whatever would you find to say
if what you love is what they hate?
With nothing there that you can share,
why ever would you want a date?

The height of passion

She's six foot tall,
he's five foot two –
they're crazy for each other.
I couldn't cope with that at all –
I'd feel just like his mother.

I couldn't cope with that at all –
I'm sorry, Tiny Tim.
I like a chap who's six foot tall,
so I look up to him.

'And guess who he was with?'

Your chap, seen with your greatest friend,
and after all you told her.
You're going through a rocky patch
and cried upon her shoulder.

She'd been so kind, she'd heard you out,
and held you in her arms.
She'd coaxed the details out of you –
that should have rung alarms.

She *surely* can't be after him?
You can't believe it's true.
Her last words now ring in your ears –
'I'll see what I can do.'

Your chap, seen with your greatest friend,
and out at half past two,
while dancing in a close embrace
as lovers tend to do.

You vaguely thought she fancied him,
and now you know it's true,
and now, of course, you've lost your man
and, even worse, her too.

Valentine's Day

A great big box, in fact gigantic –
I thought, how lovely, so romantic!
Until I started to undo it,
and then discovered that you blew it.

An outer box, then several more,
a load of litter on the floor.
All packaging, the usual con –
unwrapping it went on and on.

Once vast, your present soon grew smaller –
the rubbish pile was ever taller.
And then – at last – a tiny bottle:
five grams of perfume (not a lottle).

And how am I to take it back?
With all its wrapping in a sack?
You thought you'd bought a massive jar –
what idiots some menfolk are.

If only you had checked the weight,
but now, of course, it's far too late.
Or did you know the bottle's teeny?
If so, then what a dreadful meanie.

Confidence

Confidence, where are you?
He's gone – and so have you.
You disappeared when he did.
It's so unkind of you.

Confidence, I've lost you,
and searched for you all day.
How can you be so cruel,
and choose to stay away?

The times when I most need you,
that's always when you go.
Confidence, you're cruel –
I think you ought to know.

Trust

Trust is a fragile thing –
thin glass,
easy to smash.
You hold mine in your hand.
Take care of it.
If it breaks,
we will.

The optimist and the pessimist

'He's not the only man out there.'
(You'll soon be back within a pair.)

'Men are useless – all the same.'
(If left alone, then who's to blame?)

It's worth the journey

Steep climbs,
hidden hazards,
warning signs,
tough going.
Smooth for a while
with glorious vistas,
then full of thorns and thickets
and giant boulders blocking your way.
You fall,
you pick yourself up again,
you brush yourself down.
You're bruised,
but you keep going.
It's worth the journey.
Love is a rocky path.

II

Getting Low

*'I wish we knew right from the start
that things would last. We never do.'*

Too young to compromise

'Oh yes, I know he's kind to me,
and so supportive too.
He's always been a rock for me
with everything I do.

Oh yes, I know he's generous.
Of course, I know that's true –
and pretty handsome I would say.
I think you'd say that too.

Oh yes, I also know he's fun –
we always have a laugh.
In many ways he's right for me –
the perfect other half.

Still, all of that is not enough –
I'm just too young, I guess.
At sixty, that might be the case,
but not at decades less.

You ask me why it cannot last?
It's as I've often said –
he's lovely in so many ways,
but, sadly, not in bed.

Cheating?

Cheating?
You suspect it,
but so far haven't said.
But now you cannot stand it
when he is in your bed.

Cheating?
Have to ask him;
can't leave it left unsaid.
The longer you are silent,
the sooner love is dead.

A friend cries on my shoulder

His sons berate me,
I know they hate me,
always a cloud above.
God, what a cost
and what I have lost –
why did I fall in love?

His friends mistrust me,
that's always fussed me,
always a cloud above.
God, what a life
I have, second wife –
why did I fall in love?

His ex-wife loathes me,
my husband's guilty;
always a cloud above.
God, what a cost
and what I have lost –
why did I fall in love?

His sons never come,
he's lost his best chum,
God, what a lot he's lost.
We both struggle on,
though so much has gone,
and dwell on what loving has cost.

Some folks are pleasant
but loads are unpleasant –

the people he most wants to see.
God what a life I lead, second wife,
and I let it happen to me.

Plateau

He's calm, contained, and always is.
I wish he would display emotion –
I want some highs, and even lows
might make for a more heady potion.

He likes things on an even keel,
the same as they have always been.
He simply wants to do his job
and have a calm domestic scene.

I'd far prefer some ups and downs,
and on occasions, giddy highs.
We jog along; there's not much wrong,
but how I'd love the odd surprise.

I need some peaks, and even troughs
are better than a pool of cool.
I'd welcome a more stirring ride.
I married him, so I'm the fool.

One lie too many

I'm looking through a telescope,
I cannot help that now.
I'm watching you, your every move –
you lied to me, and how.

I'm looking through a telescope,
and what I sometimes see
is someone whom I love much less
because you lied to me.

I'm looking through a telescope,
I've got you in my sights,
and no, I'll never put it down,
or else it's sleepless nights.

I'm looking through a telescope,
there's nothing I won't see.
I'm watching you and all you do
because you lied to me.

I'm looking through a telescope,
there's nothing that I miss –
except the trust I used to have.
I can't go on like this.

We find out in the oddest ways

A letter opened by mistake
to thank him for a watch:
a Rolex too, and clearly new,
not something like a Swatch.

What's more, we're short of money,
I have to pay my way,
and rather more than he does –
he's pretty broke today.

His secretary's father
has sent him two long pages.
It's obvious what's happening –
suspected it for ages.

'Our warmest thanks for coming.
How nice, at last, to meet.
We'd heard so much about you –
my birthday was a treat.

And what a stunning present!
It truly made my day.
And so supremely generous –
whatever can I say?

My daughter often told us
she'd met a lovely man.
Do come and stay more often –
just tell us when you can.'

It's weird how you discover.
One day, the oddest thing
confirms your long suspicions
and tells you everything.

You must think I'm stupid

I'm not a fool – you phone at eight
to say the meeting's running late,
and then you tell me, yet again,
'I'll try and make it home by ten.'

Oh yes, two other glaring clues –
you've bought yourself some smarter shoes
and splashed out on a suit or two;
that's something that you never do.

You've even bought a tie in pink –
a colour that you used to think
might somehow say that you were gay.
That doesn't worry you today.

It's odd the way that you behave –
you've started using aftershave
and watching late shows on TV –
you've never once done that with me.

Your music tastes have changed as well –
you used to find all opera hell,
but now it's Verdi late at night
long after I've switched off the light.

And when I go to bed alone,
I know you always take your phone
and sit for ages on the loo,
though God knows whom you're talking to.

And what am I supposed to do?
Say nothing and put up with you,
and hope that time will sort things out
and wonder if you'll stick about?

Hell, no, I'll force myself to speak,
and do it soon, this very week.
But am I making some mistake?
Of course I'm not, for heaven's sake.

He doesn't notice

These days you never notice me
as much as what is on TV.
You only see what's on your plate,
but very little else of late.

Like furniture, I've grown familiar.
Familiar, I'm invisible.
It's part of loving, noticing –
the two are indivisible.

You never notice what I wear
or notice me with nothing on.
You never notice me at all –
and won't, until the day I've gone.

'I'm not your slave'

I've had it, I'm fed up, exhausted,
I've had it, looking after you.
Cooking, cleaning, endless slaving –
that's all I ever seem to do.
I'm not your cook, I'm not your slave,
and this time I have had enough.
So now you'll have to get a maid,
and if you can't afford one, tough.

If only we knew from the start

Some lucky women share a bed
with someone fifty, sixty years,
and never get fed up with them
or see the whole thing end in tears.

But most will reach the comfort zone
or end up sleeping on their own,
or else get a divorce of course
and also go to bed alone.

I guess we have to take a chance –
there's little else that we can do.
I wish we knew right from the start
that things would last. We never do.

III

Getting Out

*'You won't be friends, deep down you know –
not if it's you who chose to go'*

'Sorry — it's over'

Don't tell him over dinner –
he'll hardly want to eat.

Don't tell him at the local –
a lousy place to meet.

Don't tell him if he's cooking –
he'll chuck the stew at you.

Don't tell him while he's shaving –
a dangerous thing to do.

Don't tell him at the golf club,
or on the eighteenth tee –

a cruel place to tell him;
he'll slice his shot, you see.

Don't tell him when you're flying,
or on the *QE2* –

just when he's spent a fortune
on some nice trip for you.

Don't tell him while he's driving –
unless you want a crash.

Don't tell him in an e-mail,
nor at the office bash.

Don't tell him when in public,
don't tell him on the phone.

The only place to tell him
is home, when you're alone.

The worst time you can tell him?
Of course, I should have said –

is when it's after midnight
and when you're both in bed.

'Sorry, I'm too knackered'

No sex for days –
and quite a few,
but I don't mind
as much as you.

No sex for weeks –
a month or two.
Exhausted,
so much else to do.

No sex for ages –
year or two.
Don't miss it now –
but know you do.

No sex at all –
you leave me be.
There's someone else,
you're leaving me.

'We can still be friends'

You won't be friends, deep down you know –
not if it's you who chose to go.

In time perhaps, in time maybe.
Not now, you'll have to wait and see.

'It's over'– once your words are out,
I rather doubt he'll stick about.

He may be hurting quite a bit –
there isn't any point in it.

Why ever should he be your mate
when ousted as a steady date?

He doesn't want to be your friend.
Not now; that's it, kaput, the end.

One-way traffic

You spend so many hours on him,
there's never time for you.
The subject's always him, him, him,
and what *he* wants to do.

Your needs are lost, they're drowned in his –
it's all a one-way show.
You try and point that out to him –
good God, he needs to know.

It's one-way traffic all the way –
his needs drown out your own.
Your problems are all lost on him –
you have to cope alone.

It's one-way traffic all the way –
you're headed for a smash.
Why sit there as a passenger
while waiting for the crash?

A cautionary tale

A neighbour's long-drawn-out divorce
made both her daughters sad of course,
and not just sad, but hopping mad
when Mum found a replacement 'Dad'.

They always blocked his way upstairs
by jamming it with teddy bears,
and begged to sleep with her in bed
to stop him turning up instead.

They called him Richard, never 'Dick',
and thought up every little trick
to keep the nasty chap away
and stop him asking them to play.

They hated him suggesting games
like guessing all their teddies' names,
and every night the way he said
'Now girls, I think it's time for bed!'

One day, they poured some Superglue
on Richard's BMW.
They knew it was his favourite toy,
and more than that, his pride and joy.

It worked – their plan was more than clever.
The next day, he drove off for ever.

Why did you come back?

You love the children, that's for sure,
but is that why you're staying?
Are they the reason you came back?
I'm hoping not – I'm praying.

IV

Getting Hitched

'Some chaps want mothers more than wives'

Too much planning

The organ starts,
and I take my first slow steps up the nave
dragging doubts and swathes of silk in my wake,
centre stage in a pantomime,
the lead part in the last act
of singledom.

A flurry of feathered hats
floats in my direction.
The congregation smiles me ever onwards
as my father guides me to my fate,
now thirty feet away.

Six weeks of doubting,
drowned out by fretting and flapping
and planning and primping
and pinning and presents.
'Don't worry, darling, it's only last-minute nerves.'

I notice my aunt in the front pew
and remember the wine cooler she gave us.
Why do you need a wine cooler if you have a fridge?
And it has room for only one bottle.
And you have to clean it out every time you use it.
And it has a plug, so you can't even take it on picnics.

This is madness:
I'm almost there and I'm thinking about wine coolers.

The organ stops.
The silence is suffocating, closing in.
The vicar takes my hand.
It's too late now.

He won't change

Few things will ever change a man –
a woman very rarely can.
They may change for a year or two,
but then do what they used to do.
What's more, if you're hitched up by then,
you'll never change them back again.

So often we delude ourselves
that men will change;
they rarely do.
They might do, for a little bit,
but soon revert, when used to you.

By then they've reached the comfort zone
and do just what they did before;
and as for asking them to change,
there's no point trying any more.

Does he see you as a wife or a mother?

Some chaps want mothers more than wives –
it's true, and very often said.
The only time some men want wives
is when it's time to go to bed.

On top of that, some men want wives
who pamper them just like a kid,
and cosset and look after them,
exactly like their mothers did.

A *Mumsnet* survey in the news
found most men saw their wives as mothers
as soon as kids were on the scene,
and, well behind that, as their lovers.

How sad that when we're mothers too,
they see us that way more than wives–
a risk I guess we have to take
when children come into our lives.

It's hard to get the balance right –
to be a wife and mother too.
It's pretty well impossible.
How many women do?

Do you?

A husband's complaint

'Is there any way of stopping
someone who's obsessed with shopping?
I often wish my darling wife
would stop and get herself a life.

And this may come as no surprise –
she doesn't want most things she buys.
She gets enough to fill a sack,
and then takes half the items back.

And after that she's off again,
ignoring me if I complain.
It's worse on holidays abroad;
she's always shopping, I get bored.

And market days are even worse –
she always takes a bulging purse
and spends loads in the marketplace,
and then can't fit things in her case.

I lend her mine, because I'm kind,
and have to leave *my* clothes behind.
These days, it's getting far from funny –
it's not as if we have the money.

I'm asking you – as you're her friend –
well, will the nightmare ever end?
I simply don't know what to do.
But you might, so I'm asking you.'

'Yes', I reply, 'it's rather strange,
but know that she will never change;
a tiny little bit at best –
they don't when they are that obsessed.

I'm sorry, I can't see the end.
And, as you say, your wife's my friend,
so please don't contemplate divorce.
Well, that would cost far more of course'.

Beware of marrying an author

They're always the same after breakfast –
they disappear off to their den,
and then throw their mess all around it
and moan when you clear up again.

Quite often they surface at lunchtime
and ask if there's something to eat.
There's nothing if *you* haven't bought it.
Them buy it? That *would* be a treat.

And always they turn up at dinner –
'So what are we having tonight?' –
and take you through all that they've written,
and often that takes them all night.

Warning – don't marry an author;
they live in a world of their own.
What most would prefer is a servant,
or someone who leaves them alone.

Not now

Something that you need to know –
'God, can't it wait?' You tell him 'No'.
He tells you, 'I'm already late.
I'm rushing, surely it can wait?'

You wait – and wait – until he's free.
'Not now, there's something on TV'.
Or something that he needs to do –
that's anything but talk to you.

Tomorrow? Next week? Months away?
You groan and wait another day.
You wait – and wait – and wait again.
Why do we always wait for men?

And when at last, *at last* they're free,
your question's lost to memory.

Silence, please

I'm gazing out across the sea.
I wish he wouldn't talk to me.

I'm in the garden, planting flowers.
He's talking, and he has for hours.

I'm up a mountain, so is he.
He talks, I want tranquillity.

I'm listening to a robin sing.
Please, darling, don't say anything.

I'm watching as the sun goes down.
He starts to talk, I start to frown.

It's summer, and we're on a walk.
Why *does* he always have to talk?

I'd love to say 'I love you'

I'd love to say 'I love you' –
at times I think I do.
But do I always love you?
No, sadly, that's not true.

I'd love to have a baby,
I'm scared it's now too late –
I haven't got much time left
approaching thirty-eight.

I'm certain that you love me –
I see it in your eyes,
and anyway, you say so
and never tell me lies.

I'd love to have a baby,
or, better still, have two.
The problem is, I'd love them
and always more than you.

Things I despair of

Romantic gestures: things like bringing
a nice big bunch of flowers for me;

help with shopping, cooking sometimes,
noticing we're out of tea;

cleaning, laundry, stripping bedding,
getting double duvets on;

losing all our invitations
until it's past the day they're on;

Christmas, all the organising,
and leaving me to do the tree,

and never guessing what I'd like,
and every Christmas asking me;

gardening, weeding, mowing, seeding –
you always leave the lot to me;

Asda, Waitrose, Marks & Spencer –
a hundred items you can't see;

perfume, make-up, what I'm wearing,
you never notice if it's new.

Quite miraculous we've lasted
and jog along so well, we two.

Please don't be honest

Please don't be honest,
I'd like a few lies.
The truth on occasions
is sometimes unwise.

'What gorgeous carnations!
Oh darling, they're great.
But flowers? So unlike you,
unless you're home late.'

'Well, a girl in the office
was throwing them out.
She told me she hated
carnations about.

She said they were vulgar
and lacking in taste.
I thought you might like them –
it seemed such a waste.'

There are times to be honest
and others to lie,
and moments I'd welcome
a good porky pie.

'Do you like my new sweater?
I bought it today.'
'To be honest, not very,
I've never liked grey.

To me, it's so dull,
like a long, rainy day.
You need something brighter –
you look washed away.

I like you in colours
like red and bright blue.
And why look so downcast?
You asked, didn't you?'

Now that I'm older,
I don't want the truth,
or not half as much
as I did in my youth.

A lie can be nicer,
so keep some in store,
because, if I'm honest,
I'd love a few more.

My husband's girlfriend

He gazes at her lovingly each day –
he simply cannot take his eyes away.

She lives downstairs, and there they play away.
And worst of all, I know she's there to stay.

On top of that, he hates me in their space –
if I intrude, that's written on his face.

What's more, he tells me everything they do,
expecting me to listen to it, too.

I sometimes think he'd love her as his wife –
the wretched new computer in his life.

Sex could be worse

What very bad luck
for a pretty young duck
that a mating's a ducking as well.
You see, their poor necks
are submerged during sex,
so the process is absolute hell.

If a female has flown
to a pond quite alone
or a lake nice and free of a male,
wish her luck, as a f–k for a duck
is quite yuck –
as she's ducked from her head to her tail.

He clambers on top,
she's down with a plop.
For her, the whole thing is a pain.
And the dreadful thing is,
at the end of his biz,
there's a chance she won't float up again.

What if our necks
were submerged during sex
as a duck's could so easily be?
Sex may be a downer,
but never a drowner –
at least, that's a comfort to me.

At least men don't treat us
that way in coitus.

We wake up quite safely in bed.
No duck has that luck,
and one single f–k
could end in the chance that she's dead.

Sex or chocolate?

Sex or chocolate? Which for you,
if forced to choose between the two
for one whole year? What would you do?
I simply can't believe it's true
that recent surveys have unveiled
that sex spectacularly failed
to make respondents as content.
No wonder that so much is spent
on buying chocolate every year,
if sex, compared, comes nowhere near.

Now, sex or chocolate, which for me?
I'd say that sex it has to be.
Of course I'm telling you the truth –
the fact is, I have no sweet tooth.
But forced to choose twixt sex and booze,
I know exactly which I'd choose.

I love you just the way you are

Creases in your trousers
and in your face as well,
same old coat as usual –
My God, it's done a spell.

Same old threadbare sweaters
and ditto dressing gown.
Same old agèd pinstripes
to wear when up in town.

Same old suit and jacket,
same old favourite tie.
But do I try and change you?
God, no, I wouldn't try.

I'm simply not that bothered
you rarely look your best.
It's quite enough to like you,
whenever you're undressed.

Thank you

You rarely give me rings and things,
but, better still, you give me wings.

You often praise the things I do
and say how much I mean to you.

You lift me when my spirits drown
and when my confidence is down.

You say I do the same for you.
I hope I do – I hope that's true.

I do not miss the diamond rings
when blessed with more important things.

V

Getting Mad

*You're almost at the checkout,
one customer away . . .*

Why bother asking?

Could someone change that light bulb,
or take the rubbish out?

Could someone do the dinner,
or else please take me out?

Could someone nip to Asda?
We're almost out of bread.

Oh yes, and get some wine in –
we're running out of red.

Could someone strip the duvets
and load up the machine?

Could someone fetch the floor mop
and give the place a clean?

Please get up off your backside
for once, and do your bit.

How *can* you simply sit there
when I do all of it?

At least, please lay the table
and switch off the TV.

How can you simply slump there
and leave it all to me?

At least, please bring the mail down
that's strewn all round the hall.

Give up. Why bother asking?
You know you'll do it all.

House of horrors

The kitchen lights are blinking,
the loo has sprung a leak,
the plumbers are all busy –
can't come until next week.

The daily's back in Poland,
away a month or two.
The ironing pile is massive –
a mountain there to do.

The sitting room needs painting –
you take a picture down.
Behind, it's lemon yellow,
the rest of it is brown.

The garden's looking ghastly,
and, just as you had dreaded,
that tree has fallen over –
your statue's now beheaded.

Last week a pot of coffee
fell off the windowsill –
you need the carpet cleaners,
but can't afford the bill.

The dryer's now not working,
it's somehow jammed, the door;
you fetch a pair of pliers –
the door's now on the floor.

What's wrong with your computer?
You can't print out a thing.
The phone's behaving weirdly,
you hardly hear it ring.

The outside paint is peeling –
it's flaking everywhere,
and if you slam the door shut
it's like it's snowing there.

The shower isn't working,
it's now too hot or cold.
You put it in last Christmas –
it's not as if it's old.

What fool would want a mansion?
A house is bad enough.
You spend a bloody fortune
and still you're living rough.

Clothes shopping

I'm standing at the mirror
and don't like what I see.
I've tried on seven dresses –
all hideous on me.

I start to lose my temper,
I can't face finding more,
or sorting out the rejects
and hangers on the floor.

I brace myself to do it,
but start to get depressed –
there must be something out there.
There isn't. I get dressed.

Oh blast! I've blotched my lipstick –
it's smeared across a dress!
But will the salesgirl notice?
It's piling up, the stress.

I'll say I didn't do it –
'It truly wasn't me!'
Or else I'll have to hide it,
and somewhere she can't see.

And now I hate my figure
and feel I want to cry,
and envy other women
who spot just what to buy.

I only do when leaving
the boutique or the shop,
but can't face more undressing
and know it's time to stop.

I see the perfect item –
it's just beside the door.
I groan and walk right past it –
I can't face any more.

Family rows

When my lot lose their temper
I'm calm, and stay objective.
I simply go all silent,
it's brilliantly effective.

Well, if you're always talking,
a silence is a threat,
and I would recommend it –
a much, much better bet.

You watch them while they're ranting,
they know they can't get through,
they'd rather you were screaming
and don't know what to do.

I button up, say nothing –
for them, infuriating.
You see it in their faces,
they find it so frustrating.

My silences work wonders
whenever they are cross.
Deprived of any feedback,
they're at a total loss.

It's pointless standing shouting
if you say nothing back,
and soon they too fall silent
and things are back on track.

I never lose my temper –
at least not in my voice.
A silence works much better –
I recommend that choice.

Do you have a neighbour like this?

'Just thought I'd drop by'; that ring at the door –
each day you dread it that little bit more.

A fellow who's lonely – few friends and no wife –
but oh, how that doorbell is wrecking your life.

You wake in the morning, plan ways to be out,
but know that at some point you'll have him about.

You don't sit by windows or answer the phone,
you yearn more and more for a day on your own.

Of course you feel sorry, don't mind the odd call,
but these days you're dragging your feet through the hall.

You have to be tougher and stand there and say,
'I'm sorry, I'm busy, so please not today.'

You *must* find the words to say you need space,
whatever the hurt or the pain on his face.

'Just thought I'd drop by' – the words you most hate.
You have to do something before it's too late.

Don't smile if you're about to be nasty

Some people have a special face
they put on when they criticise.
They fix a smile upon their lips
but not a smile around their eyes,
then, wham, they're piling into you,
still smiling in that awful way.
Of course, you're free to criticise,
but please, please, put that smile away.

'Just bring a bottle'

A birthday of a friend of mine:
'Don't bring a present, just some wine,
and if you truly wouldn't mind
a special one would be most kind!'

I hand it over at the door
and never see it any more.
There's wine on offer, three quid stuff,
by ten o'clock I've drunk enough.

Now what am I supposed to do?
I'd spent a bloody fortune too,
and so has every other guest.
I keep my silence like the rest.

We can't ask for our bottles back –
they're now upon our neighbour's rack.
We never guessed the crafty fella
was planning to top up his cellar.

Attention-seekers

How irritating kids can be,
with constant cries of 'Look at me!'
At least a dozen times a day,
'Mummy, look at me!' they'll say.

In the garden, up the tree –
'Mummy, Mummy, look at me.
Can you see how high we are?
Mummy, look – we've got this far!'

In the sea or swimming pool,
in the pantomime at school,
'Mummy, Mummy, look at me!
Mummy, Mummy, did you see?'

Every breakfast, lunch and tea –
'Mummy, Mummy – look at me!
LOOK AT ME! YOU HAVEN'T LOOKED!'
'I will, as soon as this is cooked.'

How irritating they can be
with constant cries of 'Look at me!'
I often pray I'll see the day
their mothers groan and look away.

Time to kill

You're almost at the checkout,
one customer away –
you need to get through quickly –
you haven't got all day.

The woman who's before you
has loads of time to shop –
you know, because she's chatting.
Christ, will she ever stop?

She now can't find her glasses.
Can things get any worse?
Oh yes, you could have guessed it –
she's also lost her purse.

At last she finds her glasses –
of course, upon her head,
but not before you've offered
to lend her yours instead.

Thank God, she's found the money –
the whole thing takes an age.
By now, you're getting dangerous,
towards the murder stage.

A credit card? Forget it.
She's settling up in cash,
and counting it at snail's pace
just when you need to dash.

You cough, you start to fidget,
you even stamp your feet.
Now what's the woman up to?
She's checking her receipt!

You're normally good-natured,
but people at the till
who cannot move through smoothly
can make you want to kill.

Doers and leavers

A doer or a leaver?
Which of them are you?
You're one of them, that's certain –
or almost always true.

Well, do you wash up last thing
and leave a spotless sink?
Some people simply have to,
or else can't sleep a wink.

Others can't be bothered,
they never touch a thing.
They leave it all 'til morning
and then do everything.

Lots of folk would loathe that –
to come down to a mess.
They have to leave things tidy.
Not me, I must confess.

Out there are two big armies
who very often fight –
the doers versus leavers
who won't wash up at night.

I rarely enter battle
'til people come and stay,
and always it's the doers
who seem to win the day.

'Leave it 'til tomorrow',
I plead; 'don't do it now'.
But still they start to clear things,
and I don't want a row.

It always spoils my evening,
I wish that they would wait.
I hate the noise and clatter,
especially if it's late.

A doer or a leaver?
Please, when you come to stay,
don't leap up after dinner
and wash up straight away.

Your local

What used to be your splendid pub
is now a mum and baby club,
with buggies, buggies everywhere –
there's one stuck right behind your chair.
And breasts on show, that's also true –
you often get a flash or two
when someone's feeding time is due.
Can't say I like it much.
Do you?

What used to be your favourite place
has now become a playpen space,
where all the toddlers placed within
create the most obnoxious din
with bells and rattles drowning out
the things you want to talk about –
unless you are prepared to shout –
which, frequently, you have to do.
Can't say I like it much.
Do you?

Round robins

They're always so puffed up with pride,
so swollen, they could burst.
Of all the letters people send
they have to be the worst.

They fly in every Christmas time,
and fly into my bin –
they never stop to contemplate
the mess you may be in.

And most are sanctimonious
and pray for you and yours,
and sent by folks you hardly know
or others who are bores.

Their jobs, their children, illnesses –
oh Christmas, what a bore!
Round robins? Leave me off your list –
I can't bear any more.

Teenagers in your place abroad

Half-asleep and dull of eye,
never asking 'Who?' 'What?' 'Why?'
Mostly blind to things they see;
country, culture, history,
markets, concerts, local fare.
Hardly ever stand and stare
or ask about a single thing –
people, buildings, anything.

Wander off? Perhaps explore?
Oh no, they find all that a bore.
And if you drive them in the car
to show them where the best sights are,
each one becomes a sleepyhead;
at night they never go to bed.

A warning: in a house abroad
most teenagers will soon grow bored,
Or think that you are off your hooter –
'*What*? There isn't *one* computer?'

Museums? Grottoes? Nature? No –
the only place they want to go
is home to Facebook and their mates.
I won't be making future dates
to have that age-group out to stay.
The only time they seem to smile
is on the day they fly away.

Pet hate

They haven't got a wedding list –
of that, at least, I'm pleased to hear.
I don't like choosing from a list,
I'd rather pick my own idea.

Instead, they have a blunt request
for help towards their honeymoon.
'And please send your donation now –
we need to book the tickets soon!'

How much to send? Or send at all?
It's such a ghastly situation –
for me, it is the rudest thing
to send out such an invitation.

I'm tempted not to send a thing,
and all at once I wonder whether
I'll spend their wedding day at home
and miss the nuptials altogether.

But then I read the words again –
'Please help towards our honeymoon.
And *anything* that you could send
would be most welcome – N.B. – soon!'

Of course! I know just how to help,
while spending a few pounds at most.
Why not pop out this afternoon
and put some condoms in the post?

VI

Getting Harassed

I wish there were more 'nothing' days

Saturday evenings

Thirteen onwards:

Please everyone, do phone me –
please everyone, do text,
please send me a nice message,
I'll do the same thing next.

Please tell me all the latest –
like you, I've got all night.
I never ever turn in
until it's almost light.

Forty onwards:

Please everyone, don't phone me –
not now, it's getting late.
Please leave it 'til the morning –
I'm sure that it can wait.

I'd love a quiet evening
without the telephone.
I'd like some peace and quiet,
so please leave me alone.

'What are you doing today?'

'What are you doing today?'
I haven't said 'nothing' of late,
because if I'm free, they'll make plans for me,
and 'nothing' will then have to wait.

'Nothing' is lovely in springtime –
nothing but daydream and gaze.
'Nothing' is blissful in summer,
nothing to do except laze.

'Nothing' is splendid in autumn,
nothing but colours and haze,
and 'nothing' is calming in winter –
I wish there were more "nothing" days.

The joys of family holidays

The Crookes and the Norrises went to Spain,
all eight in a four by four.
The day was sunny; with plenty of money
they dreamed of the joys in store.

The Crookes looked up to the skies above
and sang a song in the car,
'Oh wonderful Spain, oh glorious Spain,
what a beautiful country you are, you are,
what a beautiful country you are!'

The Crookes and the Norrises went to Spain –
to a beautiful house in a bay,
but rather than sun and plenty of fun,
it was hell from the very first day.

The weather went cool, then over the pool
mosquitoes arrived like a curse.
Peter was smitten and dreadfully bitten
and things went from ghastly to worse.

The kids loathed each other, were rude to each mother
and none of them wanted to play.
Then Thomas grew bored with Timmy, his brother,
for crying and getting his way.

And now came the rain, not normal in Spain,
the children were all stuck inside.
And one little dear fell ill with diarrhoea –
a shellfish, the first one he'd tried.

The Crookes looked up to the skies above
and poured themselves gin at the bar.
'Oh miserable Spain, oh miserable Spain,
what a miserable country you are, you are,
what a miserable country you are!'

Then Timmy, the fool, threw toys in the pool,
which ruined the lining inside,
so, owing to him, they now couldn't swim,
or scoot down the swimming pool slide.

The swimming pool flood resulted in mud
which gushed through the patio doors,
and meant filling stacks of big heavy sacks
to stop it from flooding the floors.

Furthermore, Peter fell out with Rita,
and scissored off one of her plaits.
It wasn't that nice, but she'd licked his ice
and said that his parents were prats.

She took a bucket, and then tried to chuck it
while aiming it straight at his head,
but managed to twist a bone in her wrist
and ended in plaster instead.

The Crookes rolled their eyes to the skies above
and poured themselves Scotch at the bar.
'Oh miserable child, oh horrible child,
what a horrible monster you are, you are,
what a horrible monster you are!'

Then, at a bullfight, the first matador
soon managed to see off a bull.
Appalled by the gore, Tim couldn't take more
and threw up while his stomach was full.

Just one day later, a nice local waiter
suggested a real Spanish dish,
but even Marbella forgets that paella
is better if made from fresh fish.

With everyone ill, they threw out the bill,
thus saving themselves quite a packet,
but started a fight which lasted all night,
and ruined the manager's jacket.

The Guardia Civil (Spain's name for the Bill)
was soon to pitch into the rumpus.
In absence of bail, the Crookes went to jail,
paella now all down their jumpers.

A crowd looked up to the stars above
and sang to a small guitar –
'Horrendo you all, horrendo you all,
horrendo you tourists are, you are,
horrendo you tourists are!'

The Crookes and the Norrises went through hell,
which never let up to the last.
'Never again' they all said of Spain
as soon as the holiday passed.

The parents repaired to the nearest bar
and sang to the pub guitar –

'What horrible kids, what horrible kids,
what horrible children they are, they are,
what horrible children they are!'

The green-eyed monster

'You're far too thin.'
(She's put on weight –
at least a stone or so, of late.)

'I don't speak French, but manage fine.'
(Her language skills are less than mine.)

'I'd loathe a crowd on Christmas Day.'
(Her family always stays away.)

'I never ever try and tan.'
(Well, redheads can't. I'm blonde. I can.)

'I never bother with a pud.'
(She used to, but they weren't that good.)

'Poor you, commuting every day!'
(She would, if she could earn my pay.)

Do people ever envy you?
Then button up, best thing to do.

It's sad, but very often true –
if they can't do things, nor should you.

Could you cope without them?

You're easy with them, they tell you the truth,
and some you have known since back in your youth.

They know all your faults, and live with them too.
And you know all theirs; we all have a few.

They're lovely in good times, they're rocks in disaster,
and if there's a crisis, they couldn't come faster.

They're solid supporters, they're safe to rely on,
they're good for a laugh, and they're shoulders to cry on.

Manage without them? Well, maybe I should,
but, if I'm honest, I don't think I could.

Menfriends can be lovely, and so often are.
But girlfriends can sometimes be better by far.

Does your daughter long to have a pony?

Like many little girls, Leonie
was desperate to own a pony.
She always thought her parents mean
to make her wait until thirteen.

It took five years of endless slaving
and finding every way of saving
to build a stable, buy a pony
and find a saddle for Leonie.

Owning ponies? So expensive.
Their needs are always so extensive –
oats and shoes and tack and hay,
a field where they can spend the day.

And that's not counting food and vets,
and boards for pinning on rosettes,
and jodhpurs, helmet, boots, gloves, crop –
and huge insurance bills on top.

Imagine then her great delight
when 'Halloween' arrived one night –
a lovely pony, dappled grey –
Leonie sang and laughed all day!

Alas, the girl's initial joy
soon vanished when she met a boy
while riding out across the moor.
At once the pony was a bore.

Leonie put him out to graze
for forty long and lonely days,
and poor old Halloween was sold
just one month later, so I'm told.

Conundrum

She complains about him
each time she visits me.
And he complains about her
whenever I am free.

They moan about each other
whenever in my place,
but rarely to each other –
it's seldom face to face.

I think they've been together
a good ten years or more,
and think they love each other –
at least, I'm pretty sure.

But why are they complaining
to me about each other,
not bickering at their place
in front of one another?

But maybe they're complaining
when I'm not there to hear?
I wish they'd keep it that way –
not bring the problems here.

'Do you think he's right for me?'

Advice is rarely welcomed –
at least, on someone's man.
It's easy to upset folk.
Stay silent if you can.

Advice is always awkward
on matters of the heart,
and when a girlfriend asks you
'Do *you* think we should part?'

If you don't like her fellow,
whatever can you say?
All you can do is listen,
and probably all day.

Careers advice is one thing,
advice on men another,
and if we can't be truthful,
we can't advise each other.

They'll go and do their own thing.
Forget it; have a drink,
and be there if it crashes –
a wiser route, I think.

VII

Getting Depressed

Self-doubt comes knocking, knocking, knocking –
you dread it coming to your door

Psychiatrists

They feel the need to heal themselves –
and do in every session –
and I think that is often why
they enter the profession.

They have a problem lurking there
that started in their youth,
and feel the need to heal themselves.
I'm sure that is the truth.

When I was younger, twenty-two,
my boyfriend was a shrink –
I had to rock the chap to sleep
and never got a wink.

His demons dominated him,
especially at night,
but in the day, they went away –
he seemed to do alright.

I couldn't sleep, it didn't last.
He's still a shrink today,
and people say he's normal now
and earning splendid pay.

Your problems work a treat on theirs:
it puts them in perspective,
and helps the healing process too –
I think that's their objective.

Leabharlanna Fhine Gall

I think 'physician heal thyself'
is often what they think,
and most succeed and pretty well.
I should have been a shrink.

Why are we so beastly to ourselves?

I like my legs, except my thighs.
I'll live with them, my brows and eyes.

I hate the lines around my lips.
I'm fairly happy with my hips.

I loathe my feet and every toe,
and make sure that they're not on show.

I hate my breasts, my size is D –
they've always overloaded me.

Don't mind my waistline, not at all,
but hate my bottom, flat and small.

Don't like the mole upon my back,
my underarms as well, they're slack.

I'm not too happy with my teeth –
too close together, those beneath.

I hate my nails: they're frail, you see,
and never did that much for me.

And now I also loathe my hair
and wish there was a lot more there.

How beastly to ourselves we are –
more critical than men by far.

Your time is up

'I gave my notice in today –
well, these days no-one's ever wrong
or ever has the time to talk.
I'm getting on, I don't belong.

It isn't like it used to be –
it's never ever half the fun,
and no-one ever has a laugh
or praises you for what you've done.

I've had enough, it's time to go –
can't face the office any more.
It's pointless staying in a job
if money's all you're working for.

At some point you begin to know
it's time to stop, not labour on –
and if you stay, you'll see the day
the rest of them will wish you'd gone.'

Oui, je regrette beaucoup

A thousand books I haven't read,
a load of things not done in bed,
apologies long overdue –
including, maybe, one to you.

A letter that I never sent,
the fortune that I went and spent
on something stupid years ago.
Regrets? A thousand that I know.

Relationships that lasted years
and finally dissolved in tears,
a journey that I didn't do,
and bad decisions – quite a few.

A job I truly should have got
and where I could have earned a lot,
my many failings as a mother.
Regrets? There'll always be another.

Regrets – I've hundreds, many, many,
and if you say you haven't any,
I'm sure you love that famous song.
But no regrets? You're surely wrong.

Regrets? Of course you have a few,
but surely what you've learned to do
is live with them, get on with it,
and each time learn a little bit.

Not one regret? You must have some,
especially if you are a mum.
Not one regret – or two – or three
you didn't do things differently?

Self-doubt

Self-doubt is someone at your door
and knock, knock, knocking all day long.
In the end, you have to answer –
you knew you'd have to, all along.

Self-doubt now stays with you for hours,
or days, or weeks, or even more.
Self-doubt comes knocking, knocking, knocking –
you dread it coming to your door.

Why put things off?

Why delay? Why put them off –
the things we could have done before?
Why is it that we hesitate,
and what is it we're waiting for?

Why don't we do things so much sooner?
Why do we often hesitate
until the day it's so much later,
it's suddenly become too late?

The simplest things

A mother gazing at her child.
A single, laughing daffodil.
Or daisies sitting in a glass
upon my kitchen windowsill.

A simple meal with special friends.
A chat, a glass of wine or two.
A recipe I haven't tried
and then decide to make for you.

A letter or a thank you card,
or even just a sunny day –
so often it's the simplest things
that sends the blackest moods away.

VIII

Getting On A Bit

'Are you a Granny?' the little girl said

A huge pleasure

'I met a chap the other day
who took me out at twenty-three.
I loved him then, I love him now –
so much in common, him and me.

Bumped into him outside the Ritz.
He asked if I was free for tea.
A lovely treat – we had such fun
recalling every memory!

Once asked if I would marry him –
I turned him down, regretted it,
but then he married someone else.
I have to say, that hurt a bit.

He's put on quite a bit of weight,
but otherwise, he's just the same.
He certainly enjoyed the cake –
it's clear his appetite's to blame!

Still, who cares if a chap is fat?
We chatted non-stop all through tea.
I loved him once, I love him now.
He hasn't changed at all for me.'

A huge disappointment

Can that be her? Good God, it is!
A woman that I used to know,
and even fell in love with once
some twenty, thirty years ago.

Once asked the girl to marry me,
I feel a flood of pure relief
she turned me down. My God, she's changed –
it's truly quite beyond belief.

Bumped into her outside the Ritz,
and asked if she was free for tea.
I felt I ought to have a chat,
and that would be a courtesy.

She's hugely overweight today
and eating yet another cake.
How can she fill her face like that?
The sight of her is hard to take.

We finish tea, I say goodbye
and leave her sitting in the Ritz.
Outside, I catch a taxi fast.
Did I once love that girl to bits?

Flirts

A flirt can hurt, they often do.
I pity wives of flirts, don't you?
Of course, they may not mind a bit –
by now, they may be used to it,
or tell themselves it doesn't matter
their husbands feel compelled to flatter,
with what they think is subtle flirting –
quite unaware it could be hurting.

Cougar

Cougar, cougar, none too bright,
in the nightclubs every night.
What plastic surgeon's hand or eye
has framed thy youthful symmetry?

Cougar, cougar, sorry sight,
in the nightclubs every night,
prowling, hunting, out 'til late,
desperate for a younger mate.

Cougar, cougar, painted claws,
with youthful face yet ageing paws
now clutched around a younger man.
Now try and keep him, if you can.

Cougar, cougar, clinging on,
afraid that one day he'll be gone,
while always spending more and more
to keep him from the exit door.

Cougar, cougar, sorry sight,
in the nightclubs every night,
afraid that she'll end up alone
when all her younger prey have flown.

'Are you a Granny?'

'Are you a Granny?' the little girl said,
while eyeing me up and tilting her head.

'No, I'm still waiting, I'm not one today,
but hope that I may be, a few years away.'

'Don't worry,' she smiled, 'as you look like one now.'
How to make you feel ancient? Oh wow, she knew how!

First time I've met her

She's friendly and I like her,
I think she likes me too.
She's kindly and attentive
and asks me what I do.

She's chatty and she's funny,
but could she be a mate?
Perhaps, but not a close one.
At my age, it's too late.

Too many things to ask her,
too much that I don't know.
I'll stick with current girlfriends –
the ones from years ago.

At twenty, it is different,
you'll soon meet up again.
Much later, it's less likely –
the learning curve's a pain.

Warning

The day you lose your marbles
when hearing toddlers cry
or frown when they are grizzling,
you're getting on, that's why.

If children start to grizzle,
I take it on the shoulder.
I don't like advertising
that I am getting older.

Cocktail parties

Here's great advice if going deaf –
just stand against a wall.
The sound will always bounce right back,
and then you'll hear them all.

That's if you want to hear them all –
but do you? Every word?
At cocktail parties, surely not,
most chat is so absurd.

However, it's so rude to leave
before you've had a drink,
so stand against the nearest wall
before your spirits sink.

Walk in and find the nearest wall
the minute that you enter,
and never move away from it
or stand within the centre.

Wandering off

I am a wanderer,
often away,
and right out of touch
for much of the day.

I always go solo,
I'm happy alone,
and don't even notice
the sound of my phone.

I've travelled the world,
seen fabulous places.
I've even been moonwards
and marvelled what space is.

The best thing about it –
I always go free.
And no, there is no-one
who forks out for me.

I am a wanderer,
off in my head,
and friends often say
I've not heard what they've said.

You're in my space

'Please move away, you're far too close,
your face is right in front of mine.
You're crowding me, you're in my space,
another foot away is fine.'

You don't say that, of course you don't –
you simply try and back away.
Unless of course, you fancy him.
I don't. I'm far too old today.

'Do you remember?'

'Do you remember '52?'
Oh yes, but don't admit I do.

'Remember what you said today?'
I often don't, I have to say.

Alas, my memory is going.
What's more, I fear it's often showing.

'Remember me?' I often don't,
and no, without a prompt, I won't.

Do I remember? Not enough.
Remembering is getting tough.

Surprise, surprise

I have to cling to every word,
afraid that I may not have heard.
I also have to use my eyes.
But here's the rather nice surprise –
folks think I find them fascinating
and all they say quite scintillating.
The truth is, I am concentrating.
Of course, I never ever mention
I have to give my full attention.

When forced to cling to what folks say,
it very often makes their day.
To other people, it appears
you're interested; all eyes and ears,
and find their words quite riveting,
and haven't missed a single thing.
And that, of course, is flattering.
And where this happy story ends
is making lots of nice new friends.

My parents

'Coffee, darling?
Black or white?'
(She asked him every single night.)

'Black, of course.
You ought to know –
we married fifty years ago.'

'I don't think asking you is strange.
It never is too late to change.'

My mother's death

It is not frightening to see her.
She is merely a vase from which the flowers have been taken.
We, her children, hold them now.

Not all are beautiful.
Some are as spiky as teasels,
thorny as brambles,
barbed as holly.
Others sting like nettles.
But I don't notice those.

I look at the best of my bouquet –
buttercups held under our chins –
'Yes, you love butter!'
Dandelion seeds blown and scattered –
'You love me, you love me not.'
Daisy chains made in the garden.
'Keep still, while I put them on!'
Walks in woods when the foxgloves were taller than we were.
'Shall I tell you a ghost story?'

Dells ablaze with bluebells –
'Look – like the sea!'
Lilies on the lake on our summer holidays –
'Watch out – you'll get your oars tangled!'
Flowers around our plates on every birthday,
and posies of violets picked for Mother's Day.

She has handed them back to us.
I have enough to look at for the rest of my life.

A happy ending

Please, when I go, no eulogy
or solemn words in praise of me.
Please raise your glass
and have a laugh
and take care of my other half.